CHECK OUT THAT BILLIONAIRE

BOOKISH BILLIONAIRES OF MAPLE VALLEY

DANIKA BLOOM

MIA SANDS

MAPLE LAUGHS ROMANCE

ABOUT CHECK OUT THAT BILLIONAIRE

He's been my ride or die since first grade... will my growing crush crash our good thing?

The one constant in my life has been my best guy friend, Cam. He's trustworthy, sweet, and his no-occasion, literary gifts blow every romance hero's grand gesture out of the water.

Still, he's my best friend. And while he'd make the most swoon-worthy love interest for another girl, I don't see him that way. Until he shows up at my library book club meeting and reads the role of the hero in the best book series of all time.

When we reenact my favorite scene, all the book club ladies think I fainted because my mail-order corset was one-size-too-small. The truth is, when Cam touched my arm, my heart stopped.

Then I discover he has a spicy romance novel by my favorite author hidden next to his bed. Now I can't look at Cam without imagining him as the hero of my own love story. I crave to role-play just one steamy scene with him, but how can I justify indulging when it could ruin this almost perfect thing we have?

TABITHA

"That man is smoking hot," my friend and boss, Amelia, says as she gazes across the library.

She's got a bunch of job applications for the new children's librarian position stacked in front of her, but she's no longer paying them any attention. She's too busy ogling Cam. Or, more specifically, Cam's butt.

I have to admit, Cam looks good from this angle. His jeans are just tight enough to show off some nice cheeks, and his light blue T-shirt stretches over his biceps as he sets down his stack of library books next to the self-checkout machine.

He's sporting a bit of red stubble this afternoon, which means he skipped his morning shave. Chances are, he had to pull another all-nighter, but he still looks good enough to—

"You're checking him out, too, aren't you, Tabs?" Amelia nudges me.

I grimace and shush her, even though Cam is definitely too far away to overhear.

Amelia chuckles. "Very librarian of you."

I smooth out my knee-length, pleated skirt, pat the stack of books embroidered on my cardigan, and push my cat-eye glasses up the bridge of my nose. "I take my job very seriously."

"Then, as your boss, I'm ordering you to ask that man out on a date."

I roll my eyes, because I know she's teasing.

Sometimes, it feels like the reference desk is our own little island. We whisper about almost everything here, from the books we've read, to Amelia's latest dating fiascos, to how Millie's octogenarian husband is secretly checking out books to learn tips for adding spice to their marriage.

"Come on, Ames. You know it's not like that between us," I say as I watch Cam riffle through his wallet for his library card. Maybe he left it at home again. The man's always lost in thought, daydreaming, and forgetting things.

"Friends, huh?" Amelia's eyes twinkle mischievously. "Is that why you're ogling him?"

"I'm not ogling Cam! I'm just... making sure he doesn't run off with any library books."

Amelia snorts. "That's what the RFID tags are for."

We spent weeks attaching the little buggers to every single book in our small town library. They hold key information that Byron—our shelving robot—uses to place books exactly where they belong. And, as a bonus, the tags also trigger the alarm if anyone tries to leave with a book that hasn't been checked out.

"I don't get what's holding you back." Amelia sighs. "He's cute. He's single. Hell, maybe I should ask him out." I feel a twinge of a feeling that's not very friendly until she adds, "And I would, if he didn't spend every waking moment with you. I can't compete with that."

"We're just friends, Amelia." I briefly wonder if I'm the reason Cam doesn't really date. Are other women steering clear because I'm always around? Should I back off? Spend less time with him? My own dating life lately has been as empty as the book return bin Byron just finished clearing, but I would never jeopardize the friendship Cam and I share.

"You really should reconsider and jump the man's…" Amelia trails off as Cam finishes putting his books in the gray Maple Valley Library tote bag which I bought for him at our library gift shop, and turns toward us. She grabs her stack of job applications and sing-songs, "Act natural."

"I was acting natural," I hiss back, then take a page out of Amelia's book and start randomly clicking my computer mouse as I glide it around the pad. "You're a terrible influence!"

"What's she trying to get you to do this time?" Cam asks as he approaches our desk. "Dog ear book pages?"

Amelia and I gasp in unison.

"I would never," I say in genuine horror.

Cam gives me that huge grin that makes my belly do a flip. I ignore the feeling and grin back. "If you keep talking about dog-eared pages, I'll take it as a sign to get you more bookmarks."

"A man can never have too many bookmarks." He leans right over the reference desk and takes in a deep breath. "Is it just me, or do I smell old books?"

I pretend my heart isn't racing as I roll my eyes and fight to keep my cool. "Jane brought in a box of the book perfume she's promoting. Gotta take advantage. And speaking of Jane…" I glance up at the *Alice In Wonderland* inspired, clock-sized pocket-watch on the wall and realize it's past five. She should have been here to relieve me. "She didn't call in sick, did she?"

Amelia shakes her head. "I'm sure she'll be here any minute now."

Cam leans one muscled arm on the counter. "I hope you're hungry, Tabs, because I ordered your favorite."

My mouth waters. "Tacos? From Tasty Tostadas?"

"You know it. We can pick it up on the way to my place."

"Sounds like a date!" Amelia declares.

"No, it's just a normal Friday night. Besties, Booze, and Books," I say pointedly, hoping she'll take the hint and shut up.

"Actually, it's not a normal Friday night," Cam says. "I just finished the first draft of… a big report for work. So we're celebrating. I even picked up some of that fancy bubbly you like."

"The one with the extra large cork? That's my favorite!" I wonder if he remembers why and hope to gently nudge his memory when I say, "Merci, monsieur."

Cam laughs. "You are so adorably weird, Tabs."

"I aim to please," I say before thinking it through and have to turn away since I feel my face flush. "Oh, look, Jane's here!"

Our coworker enters through the sliding glass doors with her husband, Bryan. Their fingers are interlinked, and he leans down to whisper something in her ear while his other hand moves to her giant baby bump. Jane shushes but stares up at him like he holds the key to the universe, while he looks at her like she's the center or his.

I can't help feeling a little jealous. I wish someone would look at me that way, instead of frowning the way my last blind date did. Apparently, I didn't dress like the slutty librarian stereotype he'd signed up for.

Amelia lets out a dreamy sigh. "If I wasn't so happy for her, I'd definitely be more upset that she's late."

We watch Bryan pull Jane into his arms and plant a kiss on her lips, not seeming to care that this is a library and she works here.

"Should I say something?" Amelia asks, even though we both know that she won't. She may be our boss, but she's also our friend—and nine times out of ten, friend wins.

Jane leans up on tiptoe and whispers something in Bryan's ear. He smacks her butt playfully, which makes me think of Cam's butt, and I'm blushing again.

They hold hands as she waddles her way to the reference desk with a huge smile on her face.

I jump to my feet so she can claim the chair. "Oh, Jane, you're glowing!"

"If by 'glowing' you mean I look like a piece of coal before it crumbles into dust, I can't argue with that," Jane complains, placing her hands on her belly as she slowly settles at the reference desk.

"She had a rough night," Bryan says to no one and everyone. Then he takes Jane's hand again. "Are you sure you don't want me to stay? I can read a book, or work on Byron's coding. You won't even know I'm here."

I look from the sweet romance love scene playing out to Cam. He winks and gives a slight head tilt. Just normal, friend short-hand for, "Let's get out of here!"

CAM

I have to admit, it hurt when Tabs said our Friday nights were "just" Besties, Booze, and Books. Even though we see each other virtually every day, Friday nights are the highlight of my week. Nothing "just" about them.

I follow her up the two flights of stairs to my apartment. Although I'm the one on the lease and I live alone, it feels like our place. Tabs decorated it, and it's filled with the funky, book-obsessed gifts she's given me over the years. I love every single one of them.

The most recent was a huge surprise—an author clock that, instead of telling time with numbers, shows a quote taken from a book for every single minute of the day and night. It's always the first thing I look at when I get home. But I like it even better when she comes in with me since Tabs is so competitive about how well-read she is, she's turned the clock into a game. It's one of the many things I love about her.

"Time?" she asks after I close the door behind us.

I read, "When he arrived it was nearly six o'clock,

and the sun was setting full and warm, and the red light streamed in through the window and gave more color to the pale cheeks."

"Easy!" she says, her blue eyes twinkling beneath her red, cat-eye glasses. "I vant to suck your blood! *Dracula*. Bram Stoker."

"Nice. That's twelve in a row, now?" I ask as I set the takeout in the kitchen.

"Thirteen, thank you very much! Hey, do you have a preference for your dinner plate tonight? You feel like sharing your meal with *The Great Gatsby, Catch-22,* or maybe *Slaughterhouse-Five*?"

Another literary gift from Tabs, plates with images of the original covers of six classic books. There isn't a single room in my apartment that doesn't have her touch. Not sure why it stands out for me so much tonight, but it's like she's intentionally trying not to notice that the relationship we have is so much more than friendship. Or, at least, that it has the potential to be.

"Um, actually, give me *The Invisible Man*," I say, knowing that if she wants to get the hint, she'll understand.

"Oh, good choice!" she says, completely missing the point. "I'll take… *Little Women*." Tabs plates all the different ingredients for our "assemble ourselves" tacos and chatters away, not paying attention to whether or not I'm listening. She's done that for as long as I've known her, and I wouldn't have it any other way.

The first hour of our Friday night hang-out is always the same, with Tabs telling me about all the thoughts that she's kept in her head since the last time we talked.

Sometimes, she talks about the books she's read. Other times, she tells me funny stories about library patrons, or Amelia's latest escapades. Today, as we set the small kitchen table, she talks about Jane.

"I mean, I'm happy for her. Truly, I am," she mutters then sighs again. "Bryan is nice. He's literally perfect for her. But I can't believe she's having a baby already. They've only known each other for a few years, and they just got married. I'd need to know someone way longer than that. Ooh," Tabs squeals as I pull the container from the bag and hand it to her, "you splurged on the spicy guac."

"Told you. We're celebrating." I silently sigh to myself, wishing I could tell her about the real work project I just finished—that I'm actually a romance author and I wrote *The Duke's Treasure*, the book she's currently obsessed with.

"But you don't even like the spicy one."

"I got myself the normal one." I pull it out of the bag next.

"Phew." She plops down into the chair and makes herself at home. At least, for the duration of dinner. Not once has she spent the night. And, in fairness, I've never invited her to, much as I'd love to make her breakfast.

"I think Jane and Bryan are perfect together," I say.

She scrunches her nose. "I do, too. They really are. Is it bad that I still think they should have waited?"

I shake my head. "No. You're responsible. And Mom always says that you can't truly know a person until you've lived through four life crises with them."

"Right," Tabs nods. She spent enough time at my house growing up that she must have heard it a dozen times. "But four crises just sounds like someone who has bad luck to me." Tab frowns as she stuffs ground beef into a taco shell.

I focus on filling two of my own. "Not at all. Normal, stressful stuff everyone faces can be a crisis. Like a stressful move. And having someone you're close to, like a grandparent, die. And getting so sick you need someone to take care of you." I take a bite as I recall going through them all with Tabs by my side.

"That's just three. What's the fourth crisis?"

"Taking a vacation together."

"Why is *that* a crisis?" Tabs laughs. "We've been on tons of vacations together without a single crisis. I'm not sure I agree with your mom on that one."

"Maybe," I hedge, "but I do think she has a point. The only reason you say none of our road trips have had a crisis is because we deal with the unexpected well. *Together.*"

That last word echoes through my tiny kitchen as we eat a few bites in silence.

Tabs is the first one to break it. "Remember the time we took the wrong exit and decided that it was the Universe telling us we should take a different road trip?" She covers her mouth when she laughs.

I think about that trip all the time and recall it in vivid detail. We had no idea that we'd gotten onto a stretch of a virtually unused highway without another exit or gas station for over eighty miles.

"That's exactly Mom's point," I say. "When we ran out of gas—"

Tabs pushes her chair back and starts to sing Song of the Lonely Mountain from the soundtrack to The Hobbit: An Unexpected Journey.

And even though I don't have the best voice, I sing along, because that's how we spent the two hours while we walked toward the closest town to find gas, belting out tunes from our favorite movies based on books, and listing all the reasons the book was better.

"That was our best road trip *ever*," Tabs says.

The only thing that would have made it more perfect would have been being forced to share a bed in the roadside motel. But even if we had, Tabs didn't see me that way then. She still doesn't.

TABITHA

"Hey, Tabs," Amelia peeks her head into the meeting room the following Friday. "All ready for book club?"

"Not really." I grimace and adjust the corset that's currently squeezing my torso like a vise. "I'm having trouble bending down in this thing."

She takes in my red, floor-length Regency-era gown. "Is it just me or does it look a bit..." She gestures at her own waist. "Tight?"

I nod. "I ordered it from a costume shop in the city, and apparently it runs small. I didn't have enough time to mail it back for a replacement."

"Maybe you should change into something else?"

I grunt as I squat to pick up another chair. "I don't have anything else, and everyone's going to be in costume tonight."

"I say this as your friend, and not your boss—" Amelia grabs a chair and slides it across the floor to the table— "book club can shove it."

I snort. Which crushes my ribs. "And what do you say as my boss?"

Amelia sighs. "That as long as it doesn't come out of the library's budget and I don't end up filling out a workplace injury report, keep up the good work."

"Can you imagine if I put a Regency dress on the reimbursement form and word got to the Board?" I start to laugh then stop with a quick exhale. "I need to... learn to breathe... in little breaths," I puff. "Just like Gabriella does. Abigail Cameron definitely got that part right. I wonder if she wore a corset the whole time she was writing. You know, to stay in character?"

"Doubt it." Amelia purses her lips. "You sure you don't want to change? They say breathing is kind of important, and you really don't need to kill yourself for your job."

"Says the branch head who works twenty-four-seven."

"I don't work *that* much. And anyway, we're talking about you, not me."

"I'm fine *and* I look good." I twirl once and the skirt billows around me, making me feel like I've truly been transported into the book. At least, I do until I have to grab the table to regain my balance.

Amelia pulls out a chair and gestures for me to sit. "You're not trying to impress a special someone tonight, are you?"

"If you mean Cam, you know we're just friends." I roll my eyes. "And there hasn't been any other man at book club since Millie brought her husband and he kept reading all the dirty bits." I steel myself and ease into a chair. "Book club is the one night a month I have a reason to make an extra effort to look nice. And," I fan myself, "*The Duke's Treasure* is worth dressing up for!"

Amelia grabs one of the paperbacks I've stacked on the table and sits down across from me. "Abigail Cameron, huh? She's the one you keep talking about, right?"

I nod. "Her books are amazing. Every single one was a #1 *New York Times* bestseller."

"I don't really read romance, I mean, happily ever after? Come on! But maybe I should make an exception." Amelia flips to a random page. "A bare ankle? Really?"

"Back then, it basically had the same effect as going topless." My belly does a little flip just thinking about it. "You have to read it, Ames. The chemistry between the Duke and Gabriella has been off the charts since book one. It's probably the closest I'll ever get to having a swoon-worthy relationship."

"Or you could always ask Cam out."

"Amelia!"

"He's hot, and you're the one who keeps checking him out." Amelia wiggles her eyebrows.

"His hotness is irrelevant. We practically grew up together."

"Well, you can still go out together." She raises her hand when I start to protest. "As friends. Go to a fancy restaurant. Dress up. See where the night takes you?"

"That would be weird. Plus, he's more of a black T-shirt and jeans kinda guy."

"Maybe you and I can do a girl's night instead? Drive into the city, go to a fancy restaurant? Flirt with some hot men? It's not like there's much pickings in this town."

I nod and smile, like it's a good idea. But in my

heart, I have no interest in flirting with random men, hot or otherwise. I may not have the fairy tale love story, but until Cam starts dating again, I'd much rather spend time with him than go through another awkward first date.

Amelia gets to her feet. "I should get back upstairs. Jane's up there by herself, and with all the tourists coming to take photos of her with Byron, she's probably swamped."

"Or she's filmed another viral video in the time you've been down here with me." I'm only half-joking, since practically anything Jane posts online these days hits a million views before lunch. "Could you let the ladies know the meeting room's open so they can come on down?"

"Will do." Amelia waves as she heads out.

I reach across the table to grab my water bottle for a quick sip, and let out a pained grunt. Oh, right, the corset.

I consider taking it off but at this point that seems like more work than I have energy for. And the ladies will be here in a minute, so I should at least stay in costume until the group photo. If the corset is still bothering me then, I'll go change.

I pick up my personal copy of *The Duke's Treasure* and leaf through it to go over all the passages I've flagged for discussion as the ladies start shuffling in. They've all dressed up for the occasion, but none of the other fancy historical dresses look like they're cutting off air supply.

Ruthanne the Brash swoops into the room and clears her throat loudly to draw attention to herself so we can admire the details of her handmade dress.

"For anyone who's read *The Duke's Forbidden Love*—

which had better be everyone—this is how I picture the dress that Gabriella wore in the scene where Ian, the Duke of Shaughnessy, realizes he's in love with his childhood best friend."

I have to admit, I'm insanely jealous of Ruthanne's dress—that and the swoon-worthy scene she's referring to.

Millie, our oldest member at ninety-one, is dressed in a floor-length gown that looks suspiciously like a wedding dress.

Ruthanne is, of course, the first person to mention it. "Milfred Baker. Is there something you'd like to share with the class?"

Millie may have virtually lived in Regency times, but she is sharp as a tack. "I can assure you there is nothing about this dress—or what happened the first time it was removed—that I would be willing to share with you commoners."

"What about the second time? Or the third?" Ruthanne pokes her side. "And who will be disrobing you tonight, my dear old friend?"

"Why, the Duke, of course."

Ruthanne points to Sylvie, who's chosen a black velvet pantsuit paired with a high-collared white blouse, a matching paisley vest, a cravat, and a walking stick, just like the Duke's.

Millie winks at Sylvie. "Turn off the light and she'd do."

"You wish you were that lucky." Sylvie puffs out her chest.

All the ladies laugh and start getting themselves in position for our group photo. Every month, we document the event with a picture that we post on the library's website. I'm not sure if it helps or hinders the book club's success, since we haven't had a new member join in over a year, but the regulars love it, and that's what's important to me.

I pull myself to my feet—which is quite an accomplishment in the corset—and make my way across the room when a familiar cough draws my attention to the doorway. I look up, startled, and my cheeks flush when Cam takes me in, his gaze slowly traveling from the top of my head to the tips of my toes.

TABITHA

Cam stays just outside the doorway, out of sight of the other book club members. He really does look like a quarterback, with his broad shoulders and muscles filling out his *"Warning. May spontaneously start talking about literature"* T-shirt. It's no wonder everyone always assumed he'd follow in his father's footsteps. Instead, he crushed our high school coach's dreams and spent his free time in the library, working on the school paper and yearbook with me instead of being pummeled by even bigger guys on the football field.

I *may* have had a bit of a crush on Cam back then—okay, I was absolutely infatuated with him—but that was ages ago. He never saw me that way, and my crush slowly morphed into the best friendship I could ever hope for.

I cross the room, trying to ignore the way my red, floor-length gown squeezes the life out of my ribs. "What are you doing here?"

His eyes keep drifting down my body as he says, "I

literally have no idea. Ruthanne told me to be here at seven, so here I am."

"Ruthanne?" I'm more than a little surprised. "Are you sure she wanted you to come to tonight's meeting?"

Cam nods and rubs the back of his neck. "You look..." he trails off as he tries, and fails, to find the right word.

"Way over the top?" I grin. "You know I always dress up for book club."

Cam nods. "But never..." He gestures at my dress again.

"We're reading a historical romance tonight."

"Oh," Cam says, as if it all finally makes sense. He peeks inside the room and takes in all the women in fancy dress, who are finally done arranging themselves for the group photo.

"Tabitha, we're ready," Millie calls from her seat in the front row.

I take Cam's hand. "Come. For posterity!"

"I'll sit this out," he says, breaking free from my grip. "I left my waistcoat and breeches at home."

"You have a waistcoat and breeches?" I ask.

"Doesn't everyone?" Cam teases.

My cheeks turn scarlet at the thought of him dressed like the Duke of Shaughnessy. I quickly shove the image from my mind and shoulder bump him. Well, my shoulder bumps his lower rib cage, while my own aches. "Okay, everyone, in position."

"Cam, you have to join us," Ruthanne calls out. "The photo wouldn't feel complete without you."

The other ladies agree—aside from Sylvie, who scowls—and I nudge Cam toward the group. To my surprise, he joins begrudgingly, in the back row, since he's so tall. I'm in the center middle, as always.

"Say cheese," I call. My phone's in position on the tripod, and I have a Bluetooth remote that activates the camera.

The entire group says cheese, I push the button a bunch of times, and the camera app snaps some shots.

The ladies shuffle to the table, moving a lot more quickly than I can manage.

While the rest of the ladies find their seats, Sylvie marches over to Cam, her attitude and expression capturing an outraged Duke's perfectly. She pokes Cam right into the middle of his chest with her walking stick. "I don't think this is the sort of book club you'd be interested in, son," she says.

"Cam is my guest tonight," Ruthanne calls from her seat at the table. "Why don't you come sit by me, darlin?" She pats the empty chair next to her with a wink. Cam doesn't move a muscle.

Millie looks up from her copy of *The Duke's Treasure*. "You know, my husband likes to read my romances sometimes."

Cam seems to take an interest. "He does?"

I barely contain a laugh, since I know the direction Millie's stories usually take, and she definitely delivers.

"He says they work better than Viagra."

Cam chokes on a loud inhale.

"What?" Millie tsks at him. "We're old, not dead."

"I meant no disrespect, Mrs. Baker." He looks at me with desperation in his eyes.

I'm already standing at my spot at the head of the table, so I have to speak loudly for him to hear me. "Don't you have to work tonight?"

He crosses the room and stands beside me before answering.

"I have some... reports I need to work on, but Ruthanne insisted that if I met her at the library, she wouldn't ask me for help with her computer for a full month. I figured it was a good deal. Permission to ignore Ruthanne's calls for thirty whole days." Cam glares at her playfully.

Ruthanne laughs. "You know you love wrangling my computer into submission. You came because you wanted to spend time with Tabitha."

My cheeks flush even though I know Ruthanne is just being her shit disturbing self. "Cam, as much as I'd love to have you join the book club and as much as I love spending time with you—"

"Oh, I'm sure you do, dear." Millie fans herself with her paperback.

I scowl at her and turn back to Cam. "I'm not sure this is your scene."

He frowns, and I worry I've offended him. Then again, why would he be interested in discussing a historical romance?

"I insist he stay and that he sits by me," Ruthanne says, patting a chair she's clearly holding for him.

Cam sighs and obeys Ruthanne's command.

"This is a book club." Sylvie raises the novel and waves it at him. "If you haven't read the book, you can't participate. Those are the rules."

"That's not quite true." I start to sit and grunt as the stupid corset digs into my ribs. I lean on the table and take a few deep breaths.

"Tabby?" Cam rushes to my side. "Are you okay?"

"Corset. Too tight," I manage to say.

Cam takes me in, and for a second his eyes darken with concern.

I fully expect him to comment on how ridiculous it is to waste money on a wear-it-once dress, but he frowns and says, "You're not wearing blue."

I look down at my red dress. "No. Why would I be?"

"Because," Ruthanne says with authority, "that's the color of Gabriella's dress when she kisses Ian."

Cam glowers at Ruthanne. "No, because blue is Tabs's favorite color."

"He knows your favorite color," Mille says. "He's a keeper."

A few of the ladies ooh and ahh.

"He's my friend," I tell the twittering ladies. "And he always notices little details, right, Cam?"

He shrugs.

Ruthanne wiggles her eyebrows. "I think he should stay and read aloud. Especially the part on the cliff—"

"Ruthanne!" Cam throws an "If looks could kill" glare at the woman.

"Fine. Leave if you want." Ruthanne's smile widens. "But be aware that I tried to install the new Microsoft family today, and now nothing is working. I expect you'll need at least two hours to fix what I broke, trying to get all the bickering sibling softwares to play nice with each other."

I wonder if she actually managed to botch up the software installation, or if she's making the whole thing up, but Cam—who's probably seen it all before, since he works in IT—seems convinced.

"Fine," he growls. "But if you're doing a reading, I suggest we go with the conversation at the trestle table. There are enough of us here to do the dialogue."

A few of the ladies gasp.

I gape at Cam like I'm seeing my best friend for the first time. "You read the book?"

Cam's cheeks redden as he heads back toward the chair Ruthanne is loudly patting. "I have."

She looks like she's won the lottery.

But Cam picks up the chair she's saved for him and carries it over to squeeze in right by me. His leg grazes mine under the table, and I feel the heat from his arm on mine. I glance over at him and his eyes twinkle. His smile really is stunning, and his perfectly sculpted jaw looks even more handsome with the three-day beard.

He's a man who women have no problem staring at, which I take enormous pleasure in pointing out to him since it makes him blush. But I rarely sit this close to him. He smells good. Like, really good, not like Old Spice or Axe, more earthy. Like a man should smell.

I lean a little closer and inhale to try to identify the scent.

I lower my voice and lean even closer so only he can hear me. "If you get uncomfortable, say the word and I'll distract Ruthanne so you can sneak out."

Cam grunts. "So how does this work?"

"Great question. I chose some scenes to read and discuss…" I trail off, because they're all focused on the sexual tension between the main characters, which doesn't really seem like a good idea with Cam here.

Unfortunately, Ruthanne jumps in. "First, we read a steamy scene between Gabriella and the Duke, and then we'll talk about their incredible chemistry that threatens to burn the library down."

CAM

Unbelievable!

I don't know what Ruthanne thinks she's going to accomplish with this meddlesome maneuver. What I do know is that she is going to pay. At the very least, I'm going to adjust her browser settings so she starts getting ads for all the things that drive her crazy, like weight loss pills and loud men yelling about how to be successful like them.

Thankfully, Tabs comes to my rescue. "Why don't we mix things up this month and *not* do a reading?"

The ladies don't take the suggestion well.

"This is why we don't invite men to book club," Sylvie complains. "We had a plan—until *he* showed up."

Mille nods. "I agree with Sylvie. If the sex scene makes Cam uncomfortable, he can leave. I'm too old to keep bending over to please men."

The room erupts in laughter and jabs at her choice of words.

"Unless it's in the bedroom," Ruthanne calls out.

Millie nods. "Damn straight."

I glance at the doorway wishfully. Maybe I should leave. I've known these women all my life, and I do not need to hear about their sex lives. Millie was my mom's first grade teacher, but she retired while I was still in diapers. And Ruthanne has been friends with my mom since before I was born—so, as a kid, she was like the cool aunt who let me do all the things my parents said I couldn't do or tried to stop me from doing.

Like secretly writing romance novels.

She's the only one who knows that secret, and I have no idea why she's so hellbent on having me here tonight. Why would she blindside me with the fact that we're discussing my book?

The room falls silent, and I realize everyone is staring at me.

"Well, Cam." Sylvie rolls her eyes. "Seems that the man gets the veto vote even though he has no right to. So, will we be reading—like we always do—or not?"

I hope my expression passes for a smile despite how hard my teeth clench. "Please don't change anything on my account."

Sylvie continues to glower at me. I have no idea what I've done to make her so bristly.

"You may have read the book, but don't think you can show up and start mansplaining it to us."

Since I wrote the series, if anyone was going to explain it, it would be me. But it's not like I can tell her that. "I wouldn't dream of it."

Tabs bumps my knee under the table. Her eyes twinkle beneath her glasses and she pulls her bottom lip between her teeth, the way she always does when she's trying not to smile or laugh.

And just like that, my irritation at being here melts

away. I can't help but wonder if she'd make that same face with my beard tickling her inner thighs. I shake my head to erase the image.

Tabs taps the table twice. "Let's vote on a scene."

"Since Cam is our guest," Ruthanne enthuses, "he should read out the choices."

I make eye contact with Tabs and she smirks, an expression that always makes my blood boil. I look away, like I always do.

She hands me the paperback and I look over the three Post-its. "Gabriella and the Duke kiss, Gabriella and the Duke argue, and Gabriella and the Duke heart. Heart?" I look at the page and recognize the scene. "The hero and heroine make love," I clarify.

"What are you talking about?" Tabs sounds almost offended. "The Duke and Gabriella engage in some hot foreplay, but they never make love."

My blood pressure spikes. I stand, leaning with my fists on the table. "What are *you* talking about? They one hundred percent make love. The vulnerability it takes for the Duke to take that chance and tell Gabriella how he's loved her for years? Her trust in him to believe he truly loves her, despite their history? If what follows isn't making love, I don't know what is."

I'm too amped to sit, so I walk to the back of the room and stare out a window to calm myself.

"Ooh, I vote we read and discuss *that* scene," Millie chimes in.

"That scene certainly is one to get passionate about," Ruthanne adds. "Interesting how all the scenes you've chosen are the *almost* sex scenes, Tabitha."

My palms are sweaty. Blood pounds in my ears. And for the first time in my life, I wish I wrote murder mysteries instead of romance. Then at least I'd know how to kill Ruthanne and get away with it.

Tabs snorts. "Maybe I chose those scenes because I think the author is taking way too long to get the couple together, and I want to know if you agree."

I flinch and cross my arms over my chest.

"Now how about a vote?" she asks. "Kiss?"

No one raises their hand.

"Argue?"

Sylvie, Tabs and I raise our hands.

"Heart?"

"Make love," I correct, walking back to my chair.

Millie and Ruthanne and everyone else's hands shoot into the air, making it the clear winner.

Ruthanne smirks at me. "I guess we'll be reading the scene in which the Duke *finally* grows some balls and makes a proper move on our lovelorn heroine."

Tabs snorts and glances at her notes. "Now, let me see who's reading tonight."

"I *was* reading for the Duke." Sylvie crosses her arms in front of her and glares at me. "But I'd like to postpone reading the lead until next month."

"In that case, I think," Ruthanne winks at me, "we should let this young man read the Duke's part."

I lean away from the book on the table in front of me so quickly I almost push myself off my chair. Suddenly, I feel like being Ruthanne's full-time tech support would be better than having to read aloud from my own book.

Yes, I know authors do live readings... but I never have. And this is different. Reading this scene in front of Tabs would feel like making love for the first time with an audience.

"You know," I wipe my sweaty palms on my jeans,

"since I didn't make an effort to dress the part, I think I should just be a fly on the wall. Don't you agree, Sylvie?"

"Actually, no. Flies are annoying, and I don't have my swatter."

Millie mutters something under her breath, and I catch the word "spank" a split second before everyone in the room starts talking all at once.

"Ladies," Tabs snaps, sounding every inch the librarian. I'm surprised she doesn't shush the group, and am really glad I'm not the recipient of the chastising look she's sharing with each woman in turn. "What is the number one rule of book club?" She takes off her cat-eye glasses and puts a hand on her hip.

Several heads drop. Apparently the wood grain of the table has become quite interesting, so Tabs continues.

"That we welcome everyone and respect each other's opinions and boundaries. If Cam isn't comfortable reading, we won't force him simply because he has quite a lovely deep voice and, I'm sure as the hero of a Regency novel, would melt the corset off any young lady."

I know she's only kidding, but a blush creeps up my cheeks. Now I have *that* delicious image in my mind... along with the sudden desire to read every steamy scene from my books to her in private. Including a few I haven't published yet.

"Oh, look," Ruthanne drawls, "he's already acting the role of our feckless hero, stroking the back of his neck just the way the Duke does when he's uncomfortable."

My hand drops so quickly it hits the table with a loud thud. Shit. "Since it's my first time—"

"You mean *the Duke's* first time!" Ruthanne interjects.

And like the idiot I am, I argue, "It's not the Duke's first time. Obviously, he has experience in the bedroom. Just because..." I stop mid-sentence.

At the rate I'm going, everyone's going to figure out I wrote *The Duke's Treasure*. And if they do, Tabs will never speak to me again. She hates secrets, and I've kept my career from her for nearly a decade. There's no coming back from that.

Not to mention I'll be in violation of my contract with the publisher and risk a horrifying lawsuit. It'll probably make the news, too, and the last thing I want is my face all over the news as the real Abigail Cameron.

If the truth comes out, I'll be forced to move to some remote town and live the rest of my life alone.

CAM

Tabs's eyes twinkle as they meet mine. "It really sounds like it's the Duke's first time. I mean, he's soooo slooow." She lengthens the words to emphasize her opinion.

I jump to my feet. "I should go." Before I ruin everything.

"No, stay," Tabs grabs my arm and pulls me back down into my seat. "Having an *actual* guy's opinion is going to be fun since the scene was written by a woman." She sighs and rests her other hand against her ribs, pushing her breasts higher in her dress. "Corset malfunction."

The combination of her touch and that view force the pounding blood out of my ears and into my groin. My body reacts the same way as the Duke's—and I'm relieved the table hides my big reveal.

"I'll read the Duke," Tabs adds.

"But, Tabitha, you'd make a *perfect* Gabriella," Ruthanne croons.

The penny drops and I realize exactly what Ruthanne is doing. She knows I wrote Gabriella with Tabs in mind—and myself as her Duke—and after a decade of keeping my secret, she's decided to publicly out me for reasons unknown. Or make very obvious hints about it, at the very least.

What if anyone else realizes that Tabs's hair is the same shade as Gabriella's? What if they notice that the two women share the same plump lips and sky-blue eyes? And that they both wear glasses?

I clear my throat. "Ruthanne, I think *you* should read Gabriella's part."

My nemesis shakes her head before I'm even done speaking, but Tabs agrees.

"Perfect. Ruthanne is Gabriella and I'm the Duke." She reaches for the book and her fingers brush against mine. "Everyone turn to page 187. Ruthanne, whenever you're ready."

Ruthanne looks like she's going to argue but then she lets out a resigned nod. "Chapter 23, the Duke's point of view. *Ahem.*" She raises the pitch of her voice so that she sounds like a twelve-year-old child and starts to read:

"But, your Grace, I don't understand. You're my dearest acquaintance, my most-trusted friend. What you are proposing..."

Now Tabs reads, thankfully in her normal voice:

Gabriella—my dear Gabs—pauses and my blood stands still. I've spent four years building the courage to tell her how I feel.

"Four years and two *thousand* pages!" Sylvie chimes in. "If this love story burned any slower, it could be sold to the temple and used as an eternal flame."

Tabs looks up at the ceiling. "Agreed."

I bump her leg and mouth, "What?"

"It's incredibly frustrating how long it's taking them to get together. But when they finally, *finally* get together, I just know it'll be forever."

Millie shakes her head. "I don't disagree. But why on god's green earth did Abigail Cameron have to take *so long* to get to the good stuff?"

I stare at Tabs, willing her to answer, but it's Ruthanne who speaks up.

"Millie, no disrespect, but I think this *is* the good stuff. All that tension. All the longing. I mean, it seems obvious that the author has lived through unrequited love."

I focus all my energy on not scowling at her, and look down at my chest. I have the distinct feeling that I'm suddenly the one wearing a corset.

Tabs clears her throat. "Do you all want to keep discussing how slow is too slow for a hero to move, or would you like me to read the hero's lines?"

I cringe because I, for one, think the Duke is simply respecting the boundaries the heroine has been quite clear about. In this scene, he's about to risk losing the only person in the world he truly cares about—and that's not something a man does lightly.

"Go on, dear," Millie says.

"Gabriella, I pray you know in your heart how much I respect and adore you. My feelings for you come from the purest of places. But," I hesitate, fearful that my truth might frighten her, *"those feelings are no longer pure."*

She claps her hands over her mouth, eyes as wide as the open fields we've strolled together since we were children.

I step toward the woman I've loved from a torturously

close distance for my entire life. "May I have your permission to kiss you?"

"For god's sake, just kiss her already," Sylvie barks, breaking the spell Tabitha has created. "She wants you. It's so obvious. It's been obvious for the last two books."

Tabs sighs and looks at me. "I'm sorry. We're usually much more respectful at the readings." She scowls at each of the book club members in turn. "I don't know why everyone is being so…"

"Passionate. We're being passionate," Ruthanne says.

"We're invested," Millie adds. "There's something so real about Gabriella and her Duke. Almost like…" she shakes her head. "I can't quite put my finger on it, but it almost feels like I know them."

I feel myself grow pale, but for some reason, Ruthanne comes to my rescue. "It's just the markings of a talented author."

Instead of being grateful, I scowl at her. She's the reason I'm in this situation in the first place.

"I agree." Tabs worries her lower lip. "It feels like even though they're imaginary and live two hundred years ago, the author has captured the timeless struggle of a man and a woman—"

"Or a woman and a woman," Sylvie interrupts.

"Of course. The timeless struggle of two people who are so connected, so deeply entwined in each other's lives, that they just don't realize what they have, what they *could have*. The depth of their relationship is every woman's fantasy, wouldn't you say?"

I haven't taken my eyes off Tabs. Does she really feel that way? And if she does, how can I keep my feelings from her now? This is the sign I've been waiting for. I need to tell her I want so much more than friendship.

She points to the paperback and begins reading again.

My darling Gabriella allows her chin to drop a fraction, but I can see the true confirmation of her feelings in her eyes. They are wide, pupils dilated so large her sky blue irises are all but consumed by her desire.

She presses a dainty hand against her breastbone and gasps.

Tabs mimics the action in the book, pressing her own hand against her tight dress. Like in the book, she gasps. Then, instead of reading the rest of the scene, she continues to act it out, sighing out a long breath then falling with her head against my shoulder.

Several ladies cheer.

But Tabs holds the position just a bit too long. Then a lot too long.

"Tabitha!" Ruthanne is the first to realize that she isn't acting.

I twist sideways in my chair and scoop Tabs into my arms.

"Turn her so I can untie the damn corset," Ruthanne barks, rushing across the room. Her hands move to Tabs's back as she gets to work.

"She needs smelling salts!" Millie says. I think she's kidding—or too caught up in the book we're reading—but she hands me an actual vial. It's already open, and I wave it under Tabs's nose.

I'm about to bark that we need to call an ambulance when her eyes pop open. She tries to scramble out of my arms, but I tighten them around her.

"Take your time," I tell her softly.

I don't add that I'm enjoying the feel of her in my

arms more than a best friend should. But it cements my decision to tell her the truth about my love for her. Tonight.

If all goes well, I could be holding her, like this, every day of my life. Preferably, without the fainting.

TABITHA

am places two bags of groceries on his
kitchen table. "So that was some book club
meeting."

"Singular." An involuntary blush creeps across my
cheeks as I recall coming to with Cam's strong arms
wrapped around me. "I am never wearing a corset
again."

Cam grunts in acknowledgement, but he's got this
far-away look he always gets when he's thinking about
work. He gets like that a lot—mulling over whatever
techie things require mulling—and we fall into a
comfortable silence as we unload the groceries.

"I wish I'd been in costume, too," Cam says, his
voice so quiet, I barely hear him over the crinkling of
the grocery bags.

I glance at him in surprise, wondering if I'd
misheard him. "You'd dress up as the Duke?"

He nods, and I try to picture him in a white ruffled
shirt, tucked into black breeches and shiny boots.
Suddenly, the Duke takes Cam's face, and my cheeks

flush. "Maybe you can join us when we read *The Duke's Prize*. It'll be out in September. I've been meaning to ask," I touch his arm—something I've done hundreds of times—but it somehow feels too intimate, and I quickly pull away. "Since when do you read historical romance?"

Cam rubs the back of his neck and grabs a colander from the shelf above the sink. "A while."

"Ruthanne's right. You do rub the back of your neck just like the Duke does when you're uncomfortable."

"A lot of people do," Cam mutters defensively. He places carrots, mushrooms and broccoli in the colander in the sink. "Why don't you sit? Stir-fry is a one cook job."

That man is going to make some woman really happy one day.

Wait… Where did that thought come from?

I stare at Cam and wonder what our first date would be like if we weren't us and we'd just met. Probably a lot like this, since we'd both rather have a quiet night in with books and a homemade meal than go to a noisy restaurant or bar. Cam is the ideal that I don't think any other man will ever live up to.

I sigh, a bit too loud. Maybe a little too sad.

"Not in the mood for stir-fry? I can make something else."

"No. You're perfect. I mean, stir-fry is perfect." I turn away before he can see the flush on my cheeks.

How has Cam not been snatched up by one of the single women in town? He's sweet, he's kind, he's fun to be around, he cooks, he loves books and, it turns out, he reads historical romance novels, including my favorite author!

I could use a distraction, so I grab a cutting board from the cupboard. "Let me chop some of these for you."

I reach for the knife but Cam covers my hand with his. "Maybe you should sit this one out?"

"Why?" I ask a little too loudly.

"I just don't want you to overdo it," Cam says softly, his hand still on mine.

My belly does a flip and I yank my hand away. "Is this because I fainted?" I flash back to the moment I regained consciousness in Cam's arms. "Look, I'm fine. I told you it was just that stupid corset. The thing wouldn't let me breathe. What kind of sadist invented those things, anyway?"

"They originated in Italy," Cam says.

"Really? How do you even know that?"

He rubs the back of his neck. "I think I read it somewhere?"

"Well, I bet it was invented by a man. No woman in her right mind would wear that torture device by choice." I definitely shouldn't have. "And why couldn't Abigail Cameron have given Gabriella a more comfortable wardrobe?"

Cam grimaces, and his face falls. "I'm sorry, Tabs."

I roll my eyes. "It's not your fault."

"Yes, it is."

Which is just like Cam. "Don't blame yourself for my silliness."

"But I—"

"Cam," I interrupt. "I know what you're thinking."

His eyes widen. "You do?"

"Of course I do. You're blaming yourself because you didn't want to read the Duke's part at Book Club, so I ended up doing it. But it's not your fault. It was your first book club meeting, and nobody should have pressured you to read in the first place."

"Actually, I—"

"Cam, I'm fine. It's my own damn fault for wearing a dress that was way too small."

"And the wrong color."

I shake my head. "Whatever. Anyway, let's get these veggies chopped or we're never going to eat."

He nods and we get to work. Cooking with Cam is as natural as breathing. We've been having Friday night dinners since he got his own place at nineteen. Even when I went off to complete my Masters in Library Science, I was back most weekends, and we hung out all the time.

I do some quick math in my head and realize Cam and I have been having our Besties, Booze, and Books nights for seven years. Huh. So much for the so-called seven-year-itch… unless for people who aren't married, it means the opposite, because I would love Cam to scratch my itch.

I look at his hands and, oh, dear—the things I picture in my mind's eye while he washes the over-sized carrot… There isn't enough air in the room tonight. What is going on?

I stare at him and he gives me a warm smile, followed by a questioning look. Shit, I hope I don't look like Chrissy did in high school when she used to moon over him.

I flash on a memory of her expression after she bared her soul to Cam and he ran from the gym, leaving me to explain that he was too busy with school to have a girlfriend.

Say something, Tabitha!

"So… heard from Chrissy lately?" Oh. My. God. I

did *not* just say that. I pick up the knife and start chopping like a maniac.

"Tabs, you seem kind of, um, deranged. Can we talk?"

I stop mid-chopping and turn to Cam. "Sure. I mean. No! Nope." I resume pulverizing the carrot bits. "Just trying to make dinner. Like two normal friends on a normal Friday night."

"Maybe you should put the knife down."

I snort. But his gaze is still glued to the blade in my hand, so it's clear he's not joking.

"What's wrong?" My voice comes out three pitches too high.

Cam hesitates, gently pries the handle from my fingers and says, "On second thought, let's finish cooking and then talk."

My heart is pounding so fast I'm sure my blood is being whipped into a thick cream. I sit and watch him rub the mushrooms clean, which drives that thickened blood to my own button mushroom that is screaming for him to rub it exactly the same way.

Cam looks over at me and smiles. Then he swallows in that weird way he does when he's nervous, rubbing the front of his neck as if he has to coax his throat to work. Shit.

He can see my feelings. My very unfriend-like thoughts. Oh my god. He can't run out since this is his house. And I'm the friend he always confides his girl troubles to, so he won't have anyone to share his humiliation with when I'm the one causing it.

Cam turns back to the veggies. His voice is low, and I have to strain to hear what he's saying. "If there hadn't been an audience, I would have liked to have read that scene with you, me as the Duke and you as Gabriella."

I stop breathing. Why would he say that?

He's horny, that's all. It was a very sexy scene. We're both a little amped, my calm inner voice soothes.

Unless it's more, my inner troublemaker sing-songs in my brain.

Do I want to be more than friends? Do I want this to happen? Do I really want to risk ruining the special relationship I have with Cam?

What if the sex is bad and we wish we'd left it as a delicious unknown? What if it's good, but things don't work out and this is the last Friday night dinner we ever have? What if it's great, and he wants to settle down and have kids and… I can't breathe.

"Screw it." Cam drops the broccoli and faces me. "I need to tell you something now. Tabs, I—"

I jump to my feet. "I'm so hungry. So very hungry. Vegetables are just as delicious raw."

I grab an uncut carrot and shove the thing in Cam's mouth, which is framed by his bright red cheeks. His forehead is covered in droplets of sweat.

Shit, he's going to ruin everything. I can't let him ruin everything.

"So," I cry, "Ruthanne was weird tonight, eh?"

Cam's eyebrows rise, and I know exactly what he's thinking. He opens his carrot-filled mouth to speak.

"Chew a hundred times. Don't want to choke," I say, trying to smile. I keep talking to keep him from having the space to. "I'm sorry Sylvie wasn't more welcoming. She usually—"

"Tabby!" Cam yanks out the carrot clamps his hands on my shoulders. "Take a breath. Relax. And stop worrying about book club. You know Sylvie's had an issue with me since eighth grade. I'd expect no other reaction from her."

He's too close. Half my brain wants to press my body right to his while the other half wants to knee him in the nuts and run. I opt for the middle ground and twist out from his grip.

I need to deflect the conversation to something normal. "Right. I forgot all about that. Hey, did you hear that Miss Barker got a principal job in the city and then stayed there?"

Cam nods and returns to the chopping block. "My mom talks to her sometimes. Did you know she actually got married? I remember her as being a seriously old woman when she was at our school. Apparently, she was only in her forties." He chuckles. "Frightfully ancient!"

This is good. Being with Cam is supposed to feel like home, not awkward and uncomfortable. He's the one I can relax and be myself with. The guy I can say whatever is on my mind to. He shouldn't be a person I feel so nervous with I might throw up.

Cam ruins it all by saying, "So Tabby, the thing I was going to tell you—"

"No, don't!" I howl, a wave of fear pushing into my throat.

"Don't what?" Cam asks. He seems genuinely perplexed.

"Don't…" I look around desperately, anywhere but at Cam, "don't forget to pour us some wine." I grab the bottle from the fridge.

I reach for the glasses in the upper cupboard but Cam is one step ahead of me. He pulls two down and sets them on the counter.

Thank the goddess it's a screw cap. A corked bottle would have killed me.

"Sorry it's not your favorite. I had to get it at the grocery store and the selection was pretty meager. I owe you a cork," he says with a wink.

"No. It's fine. Totally okay. No problem. All good," I blubber.

Our cork bowl is almost full, and years ago, when Cam first moved out and I brought him his first bottle of wine as a housewarming gift, he dropped the cork in the very bowl it's still in and promised that when the first cork overflowed the bowl, we'd go on a vineyard tour in southern France.

I'm staring at the bowl of corks, mesmerized, as I pour the wine, which splashes over the side.

Cam grabs a paper towel and cleans up the mess, and I take a large gulp.

"Tabs, I was going to say—"

I tip back the glass and down it. I can't stop where this is headed, but maybe if I'm drunk I won't remember and things can go back to normal tomorrow.

"—that is, Abigail Cameron… um… finished book five and I have an advance reader copy."

I'm so shocked I spit a mouthful of wine all over Cam.

CAM

Tabby gapes at me. "Wait. What?"

Then she squeals and claps her hands together. She bounces on her toes. Then she bends over, clutching her chest. When she stands, her pupils are so dilated—and she's acting so weird—I worry the corset has done more damage than she's willing to admit.

"How?" she grabs me by my wet T-shirt then grimaces. "I'm sorry."

I take her hands in mine. "Breathe," I say, as much for myself as to get her to calm down.

Fear is just excitement without the breath, I tell myself. I'm going to tell her. This is it. The book club ladies said the Duke should grow some balls, and he's about to.

First, I'll admit that I love her and always have. Then, assuming she feels the same way, I'll come clean about being Abigail Cameron. Tonight made it crystal clear that taking the next step with Tabs is more important to me than signing a new contract with the publisher.

We inhale and exhale together three times. She's finally looking less crazed.

"Cam, you *can't* have a copy. The publisher always sends ARCs to the library, but we haven't gotten them yet. There hasn't even been a release date announcement. All we've heard is that it'll be sometime in September."

"Well..." I grab my glass of wine to wet my throat, which is suddenly drier than snuff, but Tabs speaks again.

"Have you read it?"

I nod and open my mouth.

She presses her palm against my lips. "Don't say anything," she practically shouts. "No spoilers."

I breathe in the scent of her fingers, and my lips part, eager to kiss her.

"I said no talking!" She presses her thumb under my chin to close my mouth. "You cannot say a word until I'm done reading the entire thing!"

She runs from the kitchen to the living room, where my laptop is sitting on my desk.

Shit. Shit. Shit. It's not formatted as an ARC, and the manuscript is open.

"No! Don't touch my computer!" I reach her arm before her fingers touch my keyboard and bring the screen back to life. "If you touch it, the system will see me and put through a support request."

The lie is out of my mouth before I even realize I'm talking. I am so screwed.

Tabs freezes. I gently pull her away from my desk and turn her to face me.

"I promise, I won't say anything about the story.

But you *have* to let me talk. There's something I've been meaning to tell you for… forever, Tabs." I lead us to the couch, sit sideways crossed-legged, and pull her down to face me. She looks at my feet and smiles at my "I like big books and I cannot lie" socks.

Then she hugs herself, her expression pained. "There's actually something I need to tell you, too. I think. I'm not sure. I'm kind of freaking out."

No shit. She hasn't been acting like herself since we got back to the apartment. I'd just been too caught up with telling her the truth.

I blow out a hard breath, suddenly grateful for the reprieve. "Ladies first?" It's an asshole move made by a coward.

She looks into my eyes so deeply, with so much intention, I feel like she's trying to communicate psychically.

I place my hand on her knee. She gasps. "Tabs, it's okay. Tell me."

I have never wanted to hold or comfort anyone as much as I want to at this moment. I have no idea what's wrong. Tabs always tells me everything—unlike me—but then I'm the rogue who doesn't deserve her.

I stiffen at the thought and focus all my attention on Tabs. This moment is about her.

"Relax. It's just me."

Her forehead wrinkles, her eyebrows pull together and her eyes get glassy. "That's the thing, Cam. It's not *just* you. I mean, it is *just* you. I mean, it's only you. I think. For me, I mean."

My heart nearly stops. I can't move. I can't breathe. All I can do is put my free hand over my heart, our silent signal to let each other know that they're safe.

Tabs mimics me. "I know. It's just, what if… " she

looks from my hand to my face, "Cam, I think… maybe… I might be in love with you."

I gape at her. "You…"

Her cheeks flush, and she starts to pull away from me. I don't give her a chance to change her mind. I yank her toward me then cover her lips with mine.

It's nothing like the scene I wrote between the Duke and Gabriella. It's nothing like the first kiss I've spent years imagining.

It's so much better.

Tabs melts into me like the two of us were always meant to share this moment right here.

Her lips feel soft and pliant against mine. In *The Duke's Treasure*, I wrote she tastes like honey, but in real life she tastes like heaven and perfection and my best friend all rolled into one.

I thread my fingers through her hair, and she moans against my lips. That sound sets my entire being on fire.

I'd read about this moment in countless novels—I've written it myself. *The Library Journal* said that the Duke and Gabriella's first kiss was the most realistic, swoon-worthy kiss of the decade, but I realize that every word I wrote is utter bull.

Reality… reality with Tabs is a million times better.

"I want this," she whispers. "I want you."

And this is it. I can finally claim her—exactly the way I wrote the Duke claiming Gabriella in *The Duke's Prize*, the last book in the series, the one I just finished writing. The one I want Tabs to read.

The thought stops me dead. If we have sex before she knows the truth, she'll kill me. I start to pull away, but she grabs my still-damp shirt and yanks me to her.

TABITHA

I feel Cam pulling away from me, and I hold on to him like he's my lifeline.

Being here, like this, with Cam is a dream come true. The moment we locked lips I realized I don't just *think* I love him. I'm madly and irrevocably in love with him, and there's no going back.

I've been telling myself that I've stayed single because there aren't any suitable men here in Maple Valley, but the real reason is that none of them have been Cam. Every date I've gone on—every man I've met—I've always compared to him.

Can I see myself reading on any other man's couch while he works? Would we cook together in companionable silence? Would he understand me the way Cam does? The answer has always, *always*, been no. Because no one has ever, or will ever, measure up.

And kissing Cam? That is other-worldly.

Whatever is happening between us is more than chemistry—more than fireworks. If I thought wearing that corset at book club made it hard to breathe, kissing Cam steals the very oxygen from my lungs.

When I yank his head to mine for another, I think there is a pretty good chance I might faint again.

I scramble onto his lap, and Cam places his hands on my hips. He seems in no hurry to take things to the next level. I pump my hips in encouragement, but instead of tearing my clothes off, he runs his hands up and down my thighs, sending waves of desire coursing through me.

Is he not as into me as I am into him?

I'd almost believe it if it weren't for the way he was kissing me, almost the way the Duke kisses Gabriella in *The Duke's Treasure*. How did Abigail Cameron describe it? Like a man drowning.

And when I arch my hips forward, grazing the bulge in his jeans against my apex, he lets out a groan and grabs my waist to hold me still—to keep me from finding the release I need.

His hands glide up my thighs, and I wish I'd kept my book club costume on instead of changing into leggings and a baggy sweater. He draws small circles along my inner thigh with his thumb, closer and closer to my core, and I think I might spontaneously combust.

"Bedroom," I gasp.

"Bedroom?" Cam repeats like he has no freaking clue what that means. Good thing I know where it is.

I slide off his lap, grab his hand, and yank him after me. I still can't believe this is happening with Cam Gail. That I have him panting, and that the bulge in his jeans is for me.

I reach for his belt, but Cam grabs my hands to stop me. "This isn't how this is supposed to go."

I freeze, worry replacing arousal. Do I have bad breath? Am I a terrible kisser?

I made a huge mistake admitting I'm in love with him. He's going to tell me he just wants to be friends.

"Tabs." He raises my hands to his chest, and I bite my lower lip to keep him from seeing my heart shatter into a million pieces. "I should be the one claiming you."

It takes several seconds for his words to register, and I realize he still wants this. He still wants me.

"Claiming?" I smile. "You've been reading too much romance."

The heat in his eyes turns to worry—but I've had enough worrying about this being a mistake. We have years of not kissing to make up for.

I pull my hands out from under his and coax his body back against mine. As soon as our lips touch, I reach between us, unbuckle his pants, and slip my hand inside.

"Fuck," Cam swears against my mouth as I wrap my hand around his hard cock.

I grin against his lips, because coming from Cam, fuck is the biggest compliment I could hope for. The man does not swear. I don't think I've ever heard him utter the word before—so to hear it on his lips, raw with passion, does something to me.

I drop to my knees in front of him and learn something new about Cam. The curls surrounding his cock are the same fiery red as the hair on his head. I nearly blurt out "the carpet matches the drapes," reconsider, and lean forward so I can slip his cock in my mouth.

Cam stops me and pulls me back to my feet. "Tabby don't, you don't have to—"

"I want to, Cam. I want to do *everything* with you."

"Everything," he repeats. He sounds dazed as I drop to my knees again, taking him into my mouth.

He stumbles backwards, but I do not release my treasure. I use my tongue to explore his hard cock. His groan lets me know that even though I don't have much experience, I'm not terrible at this. And that makes me moan in happiness, which somehow makes Cam even harder.

He tastes salty and smells deliciously like Cam—my best friend and love of my life and now lover all rolled into one.

Cam moans but pulls away and lifts me to my feet.

"Bed," he growls.

It's the sexiest thing I've ever heard.

But we don't move. He drags down my leggings in one smooth motion, and I barely have time to gasp before his finger is in my panties.

"You're so wet." His tone is filled with amazement.

"For you."

His finger grazes my clit. I bite my knuckle to keep from crying out. His movement is slow, focused, painful in the most pleasurable way. I watch him as he teases me, his tongue playing against his teeth in the same motion as his finger. I am on full display, and the hunger in his eyes increases the throbbing between my thighs.

"Please, Cam."

He looks into my eyes, and mouths, "I fucking love you."

I shatter against his fingers. The contractions ricochet through me, and I buck against his hand. He pushes a finger inside me, and I cling to him as my body squeezes around him. It's too much and yet not enough.

Panting, I grab his hand to stop him. "More."

Cam gathers me into his arms and carries me to his bed. I collapse and watch him hesitate with his hand on the waistband of his jeans.

"I don't have a condom." His tone is a combination of frustration and panic.

"I'm on the pill."

The hunger in his eyes retreats. "Oh. I didn't know…"

I know exactly what he's thinking. "For heavy periods. Not for birth control. But, I mean, that works in this situation."

He hesitates for a second before pulling down his jeans and boxers.

"I want you. I want to claim you," he says again.

I can't help smiling at his Regency words. "I want to be claimed by you." I pause then add, "Duke."

"Fuck me," he exhales as he lies beside me. Beside me. Not on top of me.

I wait for several seconds for him to make a move. But his hand is hovering over my body as though it's some kind of divining rod and he's trying to find water.

"What are you doing?" I demand. "Touch me."

I press his hand to my lower belly and reach for his cock.

"I want to take it slow." He bites his lower lip. His nostrils flare. "I want this to be memorable. Perfect." He leans toward me and kisses my neck.

I tilt my head to give him more of my flesh. My nipples are hard and aching. I want him to take them in his mouth, but he stops at my collarbone.

"Cam," I know I sound desperate and I don't care. "Please. I want this."

He holds up one finger. "Just a minute."

"No! No more minutes. I want you. Inside me. Now."

I press his shoulders down so he has to twist onto his back, and straddle him. His hard-on is standing straight up, exactly where and how I want it, and I slide him inside me in one slippery thrust.

"Fuck, Tabs. This is… you are… " He seems at a loss for words.

I lean forward and kiss his chest. His groan sends a rush of heat straight down to my core and into my heart.

"I love you, Cam," I whisper. "So much."

"I love you, too, Tabs," he says reverently, like he still can't believe this is happening. I understand the feeling completely.

He grabs my hips, and I shift my weight on my knees. I place a hand on his muscular chest and rock up and down, his cock sliding in and out of me.

I swear that one motion reaches every cell in my body. Just knowing that I'm here, with this man—with Cam—means everything to me, and I'm lost in a feeling like nothing else.

The physical pleasure is incomparable, but it's so much more. When he opens his eyes and catches mine, I feel the connection straight into my soul. The electricity amplifies and the orgasm that's been building takes control. I lose it, bucking my hips, grabbing my own breasts while I writhe and grind on his amazing cock. I come hard and loud and with so much energy I don't think any other orgasm will ever compare.

Cam's shout echoes through the room, and that sound coupled with the feeling of his cock inside me as he comes is enough to send another orgasm coursing through me.

I sag against him, completely spent, and he wraps his arms right around me, sitting up with me still clenching around him.

"That," Cam pants, staring at me, wide-eyed, and says nothing more.

"That," I repeat, breathing just as hard, "was," I pause again, because I don't know what the word that I'm feeling is.

We sit like this, chests heaving together, his cock slowly retreating until I can barely feel him inside me anymore. Finally, it comes to me.

"Transcendent," I say.

I lean back to see his expression. His brow wrinkles and he looks confused. Pained even.

"No," Cam shakes his head. "That—was all wrong."

CAM

abs gasps and tries to pull away. "Let me go," she snarls.

I pull her closer, so tight I can feel her heartbeat against my sweaty chest. "No."

She struggles. As much as I hate restraining her, I cannot release her before she understands what I said. Before she knows the truth. Then, if she still wants to bolt, which she very well may, I'll give her all the space she needs.

"That's not what I meant, Tabs. Please, stop fighting me. Let me explain."

She finally stops struggling, but the hurt expression on her face makes my heart ache.

I loosen my hold and place my now free hand over her heart. "I need to show you something."

"Okay…" she says tentatively.

I open the drawer to my bedside table and pull out a journal, gripping it like it might fly out of my hand and escape on its own. "There's something I want you to see."

I hold it out to her but don't let go when she takes hold of it. "I'm sorry I've kept this from you for so long. I hope you'll understand."

I release my grip and the journal slips from my fingers, and I know there's no turning back.

I don't take my eyes off the woman who has been the inspiration of virtually every word I've written in my daily morning pages practice. Words, feelings and fantasies I have in the precious moments before my brain fully engages and starts to think, question, and edit how my body feels.

She opens the journal to the first page. It's dated from about four months ago. Of course, I can't remember what I wrote on that day—or any day—but I know that she'll see her name. I know that she'll read something that *just* a best friend should never write about or feel for his ride or die.

I can't read her reaction. It seems too calm. Almost disconnected. Tabs reads silently, her lips moving ever so slightly, the way they do when she's lost in a story.

Does she not understand that I've just torn out my heart and placed it in her hand? I dare not make a sound.

She flips to the last page with my handwriting on it; yesterday morning's entry where I'd written that I was thinking of telling her how I feel.

"You were going to tell me you love me," she whispers. "Even if I didn't say anything today."

I nod.

"How long?" That's all she says, in her normal Tabs voice. "Cam, how long have you felt this way?"

I shrug. "Years."

"How many?"

"Many."

She opens my journal again. "I don't even know where to start."

"Well, I guess first maybe you could tell me you're relieved that we feel the same way about each other?"

She nods. "I guess. I mean, yes. I am relieved." She smiles with her eyes. "And I want to come back to that, but this," she points at the journal, flipped open to a few weeks ago, "the way you're writing—in your journal—it reads like a romance novel. Which suggests that you've been reading romance all along and never told me. Why?"

And there it is. The perfect opportunity to tell Tabs the truth, the whole truth, and nothing but the heart-stopping, terrifying, likely friend-ending truth.

"You know that's not something to be embarrassed about, right?"

I grimace. "I was afraid of everything I could lose if you knew."

Tabs frowns. "What do you mean?"

My blood is rushing so loudly in my ears it drowns out my thoughts.

She lays her hand on my thigh, and my abdomen tenses. We're both still naked, and for a split second, I consider stalling this discussion with round two. Until Tabs asks, "That you secretly read romance? Or that you've secretly been in love with me for years?" and I know I have to tell her the truth.

"Neither. There's more. And it will explain my reaction—which I'm so sorry for. I didn't mean what we just did, what we had, what we *have* is wrong. It was everything, Tabs. *Everything.*" I pause. "What I meant was…"

She nudges me. "What?"

I hold her face and kiss her on the mouth. "I have one more thing you need to see. I'll be right back."

If I tell her, I'll breach the anonymity clause in my contract with the publisher. If they learn about it, it will be career-ending. But I'd rather give up my income than give up Tabs. I should have told her years ago.

I pull my laptop, and the journal with the pages I'd drawn inspiration from for book five, off my desk. The journal is flagged with at least twenty Post-it notes. I flip to the page I want her to see as I walk back to the bedroom.

Tabs is sitting exactly how I left her, reading another page from my most recent journal. She places it on the bedside table, then wipes a tear from her cheek. I hate that I've upset her—especially in the precious minutes after making love. I should have kept my mouth shut about my expectations for our first time.

"It was transcendent, Tabs. It was next level. It was perfect."

"Then why did you say—?"

I hold out the dog-eared journal. "Read this. Please."

I watch as she reads scribbled notes about a couple making love. It's mechanical. A rough, first draft. And it uses only the character's first letters to indicate who is doing what to whom, which means that Ian, the Duke, is written as "I."

Tabs swipes the tear away and shoves the journal back at me. "So, you had sex with some woman whose name starts with G. Why are you showing me this? Because sex with G was boring?"

I just stare at her in speechless confusion.

Tabs scrambles to her feet, and I have to hold her to keep her from bolting.

"No. That's not me. It's the Duke and Gabriella."

"As if! You think I'm going to believe you're writing fanfic in your journal? Please. You can lie better than that, Cam."

"I'm going to let you go so you can read from my laptop. But you have to promise that you'll let me explain before you kill me."

I sit beside her in the bed and find the passage I'm looking for in the manuscript. I pass my laptop to Tabs, who silently takes it. She reads quietly, scrolling through two or three pages. And hands it back to me without saying a single word.

"That is how I envisioned our first time. That's why I said it wasn't right, because I'd built up this whole fantasy of how it would go. But Tabs, the reality was a hundred, a thousand times better than the way I'd pictured it. When I said it was all wrong, what I meant was this," I poke my monitor, "the draft, my manuscript, was all wrong."

I wait. Let her process. Thank my lucky stars that she didn't throw my laptop at the wall or strangle me to death.

"You're telling me you wanted our first time making love to follow some fan fiction you wrote about imaginary characters from a romance novel?"

"Not exactly. I'm telling you I wrote the Duke and Gabriella's first time how I imagined ours would be, and now I'm going to have to re-write it."

Her reaction is, yet again, not what I expected. She laughs. She laughs so hard her sad tears turn to gleeful tears, and I realize she still doesn't understand.

"Tabs, I am Abigail Cameron. Abigail Cameron is my pen name. I'm not a computer tech. I'm a romance author."

TABITHA

*T*try to focus on the cart of brand-new romance novels I'm adding to the collection. Usually, getting to be the first person to handle new books—and especially romance books—is my favorite part of the job.

Today, I wish I was back in bed with a tub of ice cream and a family pack of tissues.

Ever since I stormed out of Cam's apartment two weeks ago, it feels like a boulder has lodged itself in my chest, stubbornly refusing to budge. My mind is a whirlpool of thoughts, all circling around the massive secret he kept from me. The betrayal gnaws at me, and I can't shake the realization that Cam isn't the person I thought he was.

Amelia joins me behind the reference desk and grabs a new release from the book cart. "So are you and Cam still not talking?"

I scowl at my boss. "I am never talking to him again. He is a liar and I should never have trusted him."

"He's not like your father, Tabby. He—"

Thankfully, a teenager approaches the desk, cutting Amelia off before I throw a romance novel at her.

She hands the boy a onetime computer use slip and grabs a barcode to stick on the book.

I abandon the cart of new books. I have no enthusiasm for love stories. Instead, I drag the weeding cart closer, the task of stamping "withdrawn" on unwanted books matches my somber mood perfectly. The thud of the stamp is a cathartic release, a small attempt to purge the hurt and disappointment that cling to me since I stormed out of Cam's apartment.

When the kid is out of earshot, I hiss, "This has nothing to do with my father." I regret telling her about my childhood, but it's one of the repercussions of being a librarian. When we sit together at the reference desk, the words just flow.

"But you're acting like Cam betrayed your trust when he—"

"He kept a huge secret from me for years. If that isn't a betrayal of trust, then…" I realize I'm raising my voice, and drop it back down to a more appropriate whisper. "I don't know what is," I finish. "He knew—he *knew* how important honesty is to me. We've said a thousand times that we were completely honest with one another, but instead…" I groan. "Never mind. I'm over it—or would be if everyone. Just. Stopped. Asking. About. It."

"Tabby," Amelia takes me by the shoulders and looks me in the eye, "you are not even close to over it. You've got to get past this anger, try to make a deal with the devil, and cry before I'll believe you're over it. Trust me, I speak from experience."

I shake my head because I know she's right.

"Amelia, I told him everything. I told him every one of my secrets. There isn't a single thing about me he does not know."

"Even the time you got phished with an email that claimed it had control of your camera and recorded you—"

"I told him." I groan. "He's the one who helped me install new antivirus software—because I *thought* he was a tech support guy. And turns out he's a *billionaire!*" I grab a few books off my cart while Amelia pulls out a stack of new barcodes from the drawer. "I thought he was still paying off his apartment, and it turns out he can afford a mansion like Jane and Bryan's. How is that even real?"

It still hasn't quite sunk in. I'd been so convinced Cam was writing fan fiction that he had to show me his publishing contract before I believed him. A publishing contract that had so many zeros my eyes nearly popped out of their sockets. And if that wasn't enough to take in, he told me he's been investing that money in tech startups—so in a way, he is a tech guy—except for one minor detail... apparently his investments paid off. Big time. As in billionaire levels. Turns out the only reason he lives in his tiny apartment is he didn't know how to tell me.

"It's like I don't even know him." I slam the withdrawn stamp on the book in front of me with a bit more force than necessary. "Cam knows literally everything about me and it turns out I don't know him at all. I thought he was my best friend and now..." I trail off as Sylvie approaches the desk.

I direct my attention away from Amelia. "Sylvie, would you trust a man who lied to you?"

"Hell to the no. I wouldn't trust any man," she says.

I give Amelia a pointed look that says, "Exactly."

"Sylvie, would you trust a *person* who lied to you?" Amelia asks.

Sylvie puts her hands on her hips and wrinkles her brow. "I'm no expert in relationships, but I do know this much: if Cam Gail lied to you, he had a good reason to. Much as I hate to admit it out loud, that young man is a good one. Now, do you happen to know where I can find that new murder mystery, the one with the red cover?"

"I'll look it up for you," Amelia says, turning the computer screen to face Sylvie as she runs a search.

They manage to track down the book in a few short minutes, and a satisfied Sylvie leaves me with a gloating Amelia. "If you can trust anyone, it's Cam. Even Sylvie thinks so."

I shake my head. "He's a complete stranger, Amelia. All those times I was at his house and he said he was working, he was actually—"

Amelia raises an eyebrow. "Working."

"All I can think about is whether he was writing sex scenes while I sat on his couch reading."

Amelia smirks and mutters, "I'm sure he was."

Of course he was.

My body betrays me by launching a kaleidoscope of butterflies in my belly as I remember how good it was with Cam. Kissing him. Touching him.

"I don't want to talk about this anymore."

There are still two hours left in my shift before I can go home to a tub of peanut butter cup ice cream and a novel that was definitely *not* written by Abigail Cameron.

Amelia finishes with her new book cart and goes back to her office, but every once in a while she peeks her head out. I wonder who she's looking for. And then I notice that the library is getting kind of packed for a Wednesday afternoon.

I cross the floor to her office. "Hey, what did I miss? What's going on?"

"Jane is filming a special episode of *Book Talk with Byron* today. I thought I told you."

I frown. I'm ninety-nine percent sure she didn't. "I guess now is not a good time to take my break?"

"No, go ahead. I'll cover the desk." Amelia takes my spot and I stroll across the library toward the stairs. I almost make it when I'm intercepted by a familiar face.

"There you are." Ruthanne beams when she sees me. "I was hoping you could recommend a book."

"I was actually just going on break. Can you ask Amelia?"

"No, it has to be you. You're so much better at knowing exactly what I like to read. I promise I won't take much of your time. Just a couple of minutes. You don't mind, do you, dear?"

Nobody can say no to Ruthanne. "All right. What are you in the mood for?"

"I'm thinking a second chance romance," she says. "Something where the hero grovels, offers a swoon-worthy apology, and the heroine forgives the little lie that broke up the perfect couple."

I narrow my eyes at her because this all sounds a little suspicious. "Unfortunately, I can't recommend *any* books where the hero lies to the heroine. You know what they say—once a liar, always a liar—and any heroine who doesn't know that is a fool."

Ruthanne gets a twinkle in her eye, and I know for sure she's up to something. "I love the stories with foolish heroines the most! The more foolish the better.

Those are the absolute best second chance romances, since the passion is so high."

"Well, if you knew the lie Cam's been telling me since forever, you'd be upset, too," I snap.

Ruthanne leans toward my ear and whispers, "The secret that he's actually Abigail Cameron? I'm the one who drove him to that publishing house ten years ago, dear. I was with him when he signed that first contract."

I almost fall over. "You knew all this time? You *knew*, and you listened to me gush about Abigail Cameron and make a fool of myself!"

"Now why would you think you were making a fool of yourself?" Ruthanne pats my shoulder.

I jerk away from her touch, and her smile grows. I wonder if I'd lose my job for screaming at a patron when it's Ruthanne the Brash. I inhale a lung full of air, but she starts talking again.

"Is it because now that you know Cam wrote those love stories, you can finally see what's been in front of you this whole time? Is it because it took a romance series featuring you, my dear, as the only woman the Duke has ever loved, to believe that you are worthy of that love? Is that why you feel like a fool?"

She places her hand on my shoulder again, and I let her. Images of all the hints Cam has made over the years that he's wanted to change the status of our friendship play at high speed in my mind and my heart. Hints he wrote right into the stories he knew I loved and would devour right there for me to see, if only I'd known to look.

All the times he's offered to take me out for a fancy night out and I've refused, not wanting to risk adding one more comparison to my long checklist of things no other man could ever do as well as Cam.

How he loved to watch me read romance books and asked me questions about what I enjoyed in the stories.

The way he always rubbed the inside of his wrist whenever I told him I had a date, that funny little thing that he said soothed him… oh my goddess… it's true and I've been willfully blind.

"And the penny drops," Ruthanne claps her hands. The air fills with the sound of "shh" all around us. "Oh, look—*Book Talk with Byron* is starting." She gestures toward the romance section.

I frown. "I'm going on my break."

"I heard today was a special episode. Come, let's watch together." Ruthanne takes my hand and tugs me toward the crowd.

I'm too tired and my heart hurts too much to argue. I follow her and hope that Jane's episode is interesting, because I could really use a distraction. I spot Byron, the shelving robot, putting away some paperbacks. Jane pats him on the side and says something to him, but I'm so used to seeing our library assistant turned librarian talking to the robot that it no longer seems odd.

Nobody else seems to think it's odd, either. Everybody gathers around, and then Jane turns to face us.

"Today we have a special guest with a very special announcement," she says.

And then *he* steps out. Cam.

"Hello, everybody," he says. His cheeks flush and he bunches his hands into fists, the way he's always done when speaking in public.

Cam hates being the center of attention, and to see

him so uncomfortable makes a part of me—that part that's been his best friend forever—want to give him an encouraging smile and a "you got this" thumbs up. I look away instead.

Cam clears his throat. "Everyone, I need to come clean. I've kept a secret from all of you for close to a decade, and worse yet, I kept that secret from the love of my life. Tabitha Edwards."

At his words, every single person in the library turns to look at me. Even those who don't know me—which, in our little town, just leaves the tourists—follow everyone else's gaze. I feel my cheeks burn, and I suddenly wish I could disappear.

Cam clears his throat, and people turn back to him. He looks like he wishes he could disappear, too.

"Tabby, I am so sorry I didn't tell you my secret identity sooner."

"Who are you? Superman?" a kid in the crowd yells.

Cam chuckles. "I wish."

"I bet he's Batman," a teenage girl announces. "He only wishes he was Superman."

A few people laugh.

Ruthanne gives me a shove forward, and suddenly everyone moves so that there's a clear path between Cam and me. He catches my eye and I see a man who's been trying to tell me who he was for years. I see it. I finally see it.

"Tabby, I swear to you, I wanted to tell you. I don't want any more secrets between us, and I want to prove to you that you are not only the most important person in the world to me, but that I'd give up everything I have to convince you of that. Everyone, I have been telling you all a lie," he pauses, takes a big breath and...

CAM

abs rushes toward me with her arms waving wildly. She's using her outside voice, shouting, "No, no, no, no!"

The crowd is abuzz. Everyone's suddenly talking over each other, and at least a dozen phones are trained on us, recording the whole thing.

I hate the attention, but I'll do anything for Tabs.

She practically throws herself at me and reaches up to cup my face in her hands. She pulls me down, but instead of the kiss I crave, her warm breath grazes my ear. "Don't do this, Cam. Let's get out of here and talk. *Please.*"

In all the ways I envisioned this playing out, having Tabs stop me was not a possibility I'd ever considered. She hates secrets. I'd been sure she'd want me to tell the truth.

"Tabs, I—" I stare down at the woman I've loved since I was an awkward teen.

I'm still awkward as hell, and a historical romance author to boot. One who completely screwed up and

68

lost the only woman he's ever imagined building a future with.

Telling the truth is the only way I stand a chance of getting Tabs back in my life. "I have to, Tabs," I whisper softly.

"You can't. You just can't. And you don't have to."

"Yes, I do. Tabs, the last two weeks without you have been torture. I can't stand thinking of a life without you. I check my phone every two minutes, hoping you'll text me. I haven't been able to sleep. And Fridays were hell, Tabs. I need you. I *need* you."

"Oh, Cam." Her eyes fill with tears.

I cup her face and kiss her. Right in the middle of the library with everyone watching. The only saving grace is that Jane isn't recording, so it won't end up in front of millions of fans.

People around us gasp, and a few awww, but I don't care. And neither does Tabs. She wraps her arms around my neck and holds on for dear life.

This is the only thing I need in my life. I don't need my career. How could I ever write again without her sitting on my couch, quietly flipping pages as she reads the latest in an endless stream of library books?

I haven't written a word since the last time we spoke—so what does it even matter if I lose my contract? Maybe I'll get an actual tech support job. Not that I need the money. But I'd rather do that and have Tabs at my side than continue writing books without the love of my life to share my days and nights with.

And kissing Tabs—it makes *everything* worth it.

"Get a room!" Ruthanne shouts. I know she's just teasing, but it bursts the illusion of privacy that Tabs and I have had up until this moment.

Tabs starts to pull away, but I can't let go of her.

Not yet. I force my lips to leave hers, but I keep her hooked in my arm. Keep her close, where I can smell the crazy book-scented perfume on her neck. Feel the soft skin of her bare arm against mine.

She smiles up at me, and my broken heart is suddenly made whole again. "Forgive me, Tabs?" I whisper, my eyes pleading. "I can't live without you. You're my everything."

"Of course I forgive you. You're my everything, too."

I pull her tightly against my chest, vowing never to let go.

"So what's this big secret?" Sylvie calls out.

So much for that.

Everyone starts talking all at once again until Ruthanne's voice carries over the chatter. "We've brought you here to make an announcement." I spot her amidst the crowd, and she nods and mouths, *Trust me.* "I've known Cam's secret for years."

Ruthanne nudges her way to the front to face the crowd. I have no idea where she's going with this, but I do trust her.

Tabs's body goes stiff against mine.

"It's okay," I whisper to her. "Whatever Ruthanne is going to say, it'll be okay. The fact that you're in my arms right now is the only thing I care about."

Tabs leans into me, tears well in her eyes. "But what about—"

"You, Tabs. You are all that matters," I repeat firmly. "I love you."

"I love you, too." She wraps her arms tightly around my waist.

Ruthanne turns to face the crowd. "Has anyone ever thought it was curious that the very popular romance author, Abigail Cameron, has a name that sounds an awful lot like our dear Cam's? If you aren't aware, his full name is Cameron Albert Gail. Coincidence? I think not!"

"What are you getting at?" Sylvie demands.

I kiss Tabs, ignore the building sense of dread, and step forward to introduce myself as the author. Ruthanne elbows me to stay behind her.

"Our dear Cam is the *namesake* and a close *relative*," she emphasizes the words and turns to me with raised eyebrows, "of Abigail Cameron. Our little town has the great honor of being only one step removed from this most beloved author who has brought so much joy to romance readers around the world."

Tabs hugs me so hard I yelp.

"Can you invite her to come to book club?" Sylvie asks. The entire crowd seems to agree.

Tabs shoots me a quick glance, but we keep the fact that Abigail Cameron has been to book club to ourselves.

Once everyone settles down, Ruthanne hangs her head and says mournfully, "Sadly, Abigail Cameron passed last week."

What? If anyone had been looking at me they'd have seen the shock in my eyes.

A hush falls over the crowd.

"H-how?" Sylvie's voice shakes. It's the most emotion—aside from outrage—that I've ever seen from her. "H-how did she die?"

I feel a wave of guilt and step forward, ready to reveal the truth, but Ruthanne doesn't miss a beat. "She went as any great romance author would want to—tangled in the sheets with her true love."

I choke back a laugh.

"You're a real comedian, Ruthanne." Sylvie takes the magazine she's holding and slaps her friend on the arm. When she raises it again, Tabs tenses.

"Please be careful with library material, Sylvie," she cries.

Sylvie straightens the magazine in question and rolls her eyes at Ruthanne. "I almost fell for your little skit, you know."

The teenage girl who said I was Batman pipes up, "So Abigail Cameron isn't really dead?"

I didn't peg her for a historical romance reader, but I'm well aware that some of my Abigail Cameron fans are quite young. And I can't let them, or anyone else, think Abigail Cameron is *dead*.

I step forward again, sure my publisher would prefer to reveal I'm the face behind Abigail Cameron's name rather than announce that she's dead.

"Abigail Cameron is very much alive," I announce, "and she will be hosting her book launch for *The Duke's Prize* right here at Maple Valley Library."

Tabs gasps. So does half the crowd. Then everyone erupts in applause.

At least that buys me some time.

And with my woman back in my arms, the world suddenly seems to make sense again. All I care about is that Tabs and I are together. I can face any challenge as long as she's by my side—and that includes revealing my secret identity.

I take her hand in mine, lead her away from the crowd, and pull her in for another kiss. At the other end of the library, Jane begins the latest episode of *Book Talk with Byron*, but I drown out her words as I focus on the woman in my arms.

This moment, right here, is all that matters. And it is a thousand times better than the happy ending I wrote for *The Duke's Prize*, which is pretty epic, if I do say so myself.

ne Year Later

I look up from my spot on the couch and catch my husband staring blankly at his laptop. Again.

It's been six months since our wedding, and I still feel all warm and fuzzy inside every time I think of Cam as my husband. I so love that word. *Husband.*

But now that I know about his pen name, I'm even more obsessed with the Abigail Cameron books. "Did you finally figure out the chapter?" I ask.

Instead of nodding, he frowns. "You literally just asked me that."

"That was hours ago." I gesture at the library book in my hand. "Fifteen chapters and two sex scenes."

Cam smirks. "Are you saying I have literary competition, Wife?"

I roll my eyes. "You know I only read other books

to distract myself until you can feed my Abigail Cameron addiction."

Cam sighs dramatically. "When my editor said I wrapped up their relationship too soon in *The Duke's Prize*, that I should draw it out, I figured 'piece of cake,' I can write five more books in the series. But without you as my muse for the reluctant Gabriella..." Cam trails off.

"I'm sorry that letting you claim me is making it harder for you to write. But I'm not sorry that you did. So... sorry, not sorry?"

Cam gets up from his desk. "Writer's block isn't nearly as hard as it was not having Gabriella all to myself."

"My Duke, take advantage now since you will have to share me one day soon." I run my hand along my still flat stomach. "And I believe our young Duke will be making some claims of his own." I press my breasts together as if they're being pushed up in a corset.

Cam settles on the couch next to me and pulls me onto his lap. "Or Duchess." He plants a kiss on the top of my head.

"Do you want it to be a Duchess?" I ask.

"With your hair and eyes." Cam places his hand on top of mine.

"Your red hair," I correct, threading my fingers through his, and picturing an adorable little ginger toddler.

Cam gives my hand a squeeze and sighs. "But at this rate, Gabriella's never getting pregnant."

"What if we act it out?" I wink. "See if that sparks your muse?"

Cam mulls it over for several seconds and jumps to his feet. "That's it!"

"What's it?" I ask, because he's heading for the front door instead of the bedroom.

"We're going to figure out this chapter, together," Cam says. He leads me to the car and refuses to tell me where we're going. We drive through town, and he pulls up in front of a very familiar building.

"It's Sunday, Cam," I remind him. "Library's closed."

"I know that," he says. "That's why we're here."

I frown. "We're here because the library is closed?"

"Yes. And you have a key, so you can let us in."

"I can't just let us in after hours," I protest as he moves the car away from the fire hydrant in front of the library, and parallel parks just down the street.

"You did last month when you forgot your wallet."

"That was different. It couldn't wait until Monday."

"Neither can this." Cam raises an eyebrow. "Maybe you lost your wallet again. Maybe we should go inside and look for it."

"And why would we do that?"

Cam takes my hands in his. "Because I need some inspiration for the scene I'm writing. And it's set in the Duke's library."

I hesitate. I know I'm not supposed to do this, but if I called Amelia and said an author wanted a tour after hours for inspiration, she'd definitely agree. And honestly, if she found out I snuck in with my husband on a Sunday night, the worst thing that would happen is that she'd never let me live it down.

We walk to the staff entrance, and I unlock the door, turn off the alarm, and lead Cam inside.

He looks around the dark building. "Now, we act out the scene so I can figure out exactly what to write."

"You want me to be Gabriella?"

"Would you rather be the Duke?"

I snort. "I could borrow Sylvie's outfit. She probably still has it."

"I'm serious." Cam takes my hand and leads me to the romance section at the back of the library.

Thankfully, the glow from the emergency exit light is bright enough that I don't need to turn on the overheads.

"How about right here?"

The aisle isn't in view of any windows, so we have our privacy. I nod.

"I'm stuck in the scene where Gabriella pulls the Duke into the library to tell him a secret." Cam shakes his hand.

"Okay, so what's the secret?"

"I have no idea. I was hoping it would come to me. I had considered adding a sex scene earlier in the book, and having her announce she's pregnant, but it would throw off the entire story." He purses his lips. "Only problem is, if she's not pregnant, what possible secret could she have?"

"Why don't we act it out and see if it comes to you?" I place my hands on my chest. "My lord, I have a secret to tell you."

I wait for the lightbulb moment, but Cam stares at me blankly.

"The secret is…" I prod.

Still nothing.

"That I'm with child," I try.

Cam grins. "I do like the sound of that, but Gabriella and the Duke aren't there yet. Maybe we can start the scene from the beginning?"

I nod. "So they've just entered the library—"

"We've just entered," Cam corrects.

· · ·

"*My* Duke, forgive me for my nerves. But, I've been harboring a secret from you."

Cam stares at me and nods. "Good. But before you can tell him what it is, I push you against the shelf like this." He moves us so I feel the paperbacks against my back.

"And then what?" I ask a little breathlessly.

"Then I cup your cheek," Cam says as his hand presses to my face.

"And what do I do?"

"You place your hands on my chest like this." Cam moves my hands so I feel his bulging pecs.

I smile. "I like where this is going."

"Then the Duke, I mean, I grab your thigh right here." I feel his warm palm through my jeans. "And hook your leg behind my hip like this."

My pulse starts to race, and I suddenly wish I wasn't wearing jeans. "If you told me we'd be roleplaying, I could have at least worn a skirt."

Cam's grip tightens on my thigh. "I wish I'd thought of that."

"I have a book club dress in my locker. It's not Gabriella's, but do you think it will help, you know, for the integrity of the scene?"

Cam scratches his chin thoughtfully, his eyes dancing as he fights to hide his smile. "It would help with my writing. Just please, for the love of romance, do not wear that corset."

"Wouldn't dream of it." I hurry downstairs to the staff room and change. When I come back upstairs, Cam's pupils dilate.

"It's perfect. Now come here."

He pushes me against the shelf again and hooks my leg behind his hip.

I place my hands on his chest, my heart racing. "Now what?"

"Now, the Duke lifts Gabriella's skirt." He slides his hands slowly up my leg and runs his fingers softly along my thigh. "What if he, I, slide my finger inside her, you?"

"I think she'd really like that," I breathe.

"Good." Cam pushes my panties aside, and I arch my hips forward impatiently. "Of course, Gabriella wouldn't be wearing panties."

"No, she wouldn't." I tremble as I wait for his touch.

"So the Duke could touch her clit right here." Cam grazes it and I gasp.

"Please, Cam."

"Cam? Who's Cam?" he teases.

"Please, my lord?" I try again.

"Better."

"So what happens next?" I ask.

"Well, I was thinking the Duke makes Gabriella come. But maybe it's better if she stops him."

"What? Why?" I demand. "I would never stop you."

"Not even to reveal your big secret?"

I shake my head. "No. I'd definitely wait until after. And so would Gabriella."

"In that case." Cam drops to his knees and does things to my body that would make a lady in Regency times clutch her pearls and collapse in a heap of silks and satins. Fortunately for both of us, the Duke and I have moved past the fainting stage, though his touch still makes me swoon.

I cry out my release, the sound echoing through the empty library. My breath comes out in a heavy sigh, and I whimper when Cam drops his pants and slides inside me.

Then, suddenly, he exclaims, "I got it."

"Got what?" I whimper and clench around his cock, having entirely forgotten that we were supposed to be role playing.

"The secret." He slams into me one more time. "I know exactly what Gabriella's going to tell the Duke!"

"Well?" I moan. "What is it?"

"You're going to have to wait and see." He stills inside me, and I let out a needy whimper.

"Cam, please." I'm not sure if I'm begging for him to keep going, or to tell me what he plans to put in the book.

"So needy," he says, pinching my nipple through the dress. "So impatient."

"You better believe it," I shoot him a mock scowl. "Now spill."

"My seed?" he teases, sounding very much like a Duke.

"The secret. Or we just stop and..." I give his shoulders a half-hearted push, though stopping is the last thing on my mind.

"Gabriella will admit she's had sex dreams about the Duke," Cam says quickly. "Because she wants him as much as he wants her."

I nod. "I *quiver* for you, my Duke. I want you to *pleasure* me. It's all I can think about."

Cam growls, grabs my hips, and makes love to me like a man possessed. "I love you so much, Tabitha Edwards."

"I love you too, Cameron Albert Gail."

I scream another release, wondering if I'll ever be

able to come to work and not hear the echo of it among the shelves.

When my knees give out, Cam pulls me into his arms. I rest my head against his chest, still panting. Cam places his hand on my belly. "Can you believe we're going to be parents?"

I smile. "I can't imagine doing this with anyone but you. My best friend, my lover, my husband..."

"...and your favorite author," he teases.

I grin. "You know it."

"You're everything I've ever wanted, Tabs. My best friend. The love of my life. The mother of our future child. And my fated muse," he says.

I plant a soft kiss on his lips. "And you're my forever."

READ JANE'S STORY NEXT

SHELVE THAT BILLIONAIRE

He created the robot that stole her job ... can she stop him from stealing her heart?

I've finally landed my dream job at a cute little small town library in Maple Valley. I even put a down payment on a house, and then promptly get my two weeks' notice. Why, you ask? Because the new hire doesn't need breaks and is willing to work for free. How can I compete with that?

Smexy tech billionaire Bryan Brooks is the person to blame, and he doesn't want my dream job for himself—that I might be able to forgive. No, he builds a shelving robot named after my favorite poet and donates it to the library so that it can replace me.

I hate how good he looks in his viral posts, and the fact that he has time to talk about my favorite books, but can't be bothered to find a shirt.

I'll never forgive him. Not even when he shows me his personal library complete with floor ceiling shelves and a rolling ladder. And definitely not when he kisses me while whispering delicious literary quotes that set every inch of me on fire. How can I ever get over the fact that he destroyed my life?

READ *SHELVE THAT BILLIONAIRE* TODAY!

ABOUT DANIKA BLOOM

Danika Bloom is a *USA Today* bestselling author of contemporary romance. Her stories have been called laugh out loud, keep you up too late, emotional roller-coasters. She falls in love with all all the heroes she writes ... her open-minded husband knows this and shows her why he'll always be her forever guy by doing all the cooking.

Danika also writes non-fiction books for authors as Donna Barker.

ALSO BY DANIKA BLOOM
The Billionaire's Shrubbery
The Billionaire's Bagpipes (two novellas)
First In: Cheeky with the Fire Chief
Second Breath: Dazzled by my Blind Date
Third Party: Merry with the Millionaire
Rhodes to Love: Daring with the Single Dad
Her Seasoned Delivery (novella)
Frisky with my Bestie (novella)
Mind Over Splatter (novella)
Mother Teresa's Advice for Jilted Lovers

ABOUT MIA SANDS

Mia Sands is a librarian by day and a *USA Today* bestselling author by night who loves swimming, salsa dancing, reading romance, and taking long walks on the beach. She's happily married to a man she met on the dance floor (it was love at first sight), but she hopes you'll take one of her books out for the night.

Mia Sands also writes paranormal romance as Mia Harlan.

ALSO BY MIA SANDS
Mile High Librarian
Mister Fit

www.ingramcontent.com/pod-product-compliance
Lightning Source LLC
Chambersburg PA
CBHW022116050726

47591CB00002B/812